DARIO and the WHALE

pictures by
BISTRA MASSEVA

CHERYL LAWTON MALONE

Albert Whitman & Company
Chicago, Illinois

For Michael, William, Kimberly, Mike, and Chief,
who saw the whale first—CLM

To my family, with gratitude—BM

Library of Congress Cataloging-in-Publication data is on file with the publisher.

Text copyright © 2016 by Cheryl Lawton Malone
Pictures copyright © 2016 by Albert Whitman & Company
Pictures by Bistra Masseva
Published in 2016 by Albert Whitman & Company
ISBN 978-0-8075-1463-4
Printed in China
10 9 8 7 6 5 4 3 2 1 HH 24 23 22 21 20 19 18 17 16 15

Design by Jordan Kost

For more information about Albert Whitman & Company,
visit our web site at www.albertwhitman.com.

Every spring,
when the sun
wakes up the land,

Dario and his mother
move to the seashore.

Every spring,
when the sun
warms up the sea,

a whale and her new calf
swim north to a cool bay.

Dario's mother has to work.
This year she is a cook at
the Salty Cod.

The whale is a right whale.
She has to swim.
She and her calf swim to a bay by the Salty Cod.

On his first day, Dario tries to make new friends.
"*Oi!*" he calls to the kids on the beach.
He kicks a soccer ball.
But the kids are playing
baseball.

PUFF! The whale spouts.
He chases a school of herring.
The herring swim away.

Dario backs into a sand castle.
Accidently.
"Hey," says a girl.
"*Desculpe*," Dario says, turning pink.
Sorry.

The whale bumps a green turtle.
On purpose.
The turtle swims away.

Later, Dario runs along the sand.
He flies a kite
by himself.

The whale has a notched tail.
He launches himself
UP.

Dario sees the whale.

The whale sees Dario.

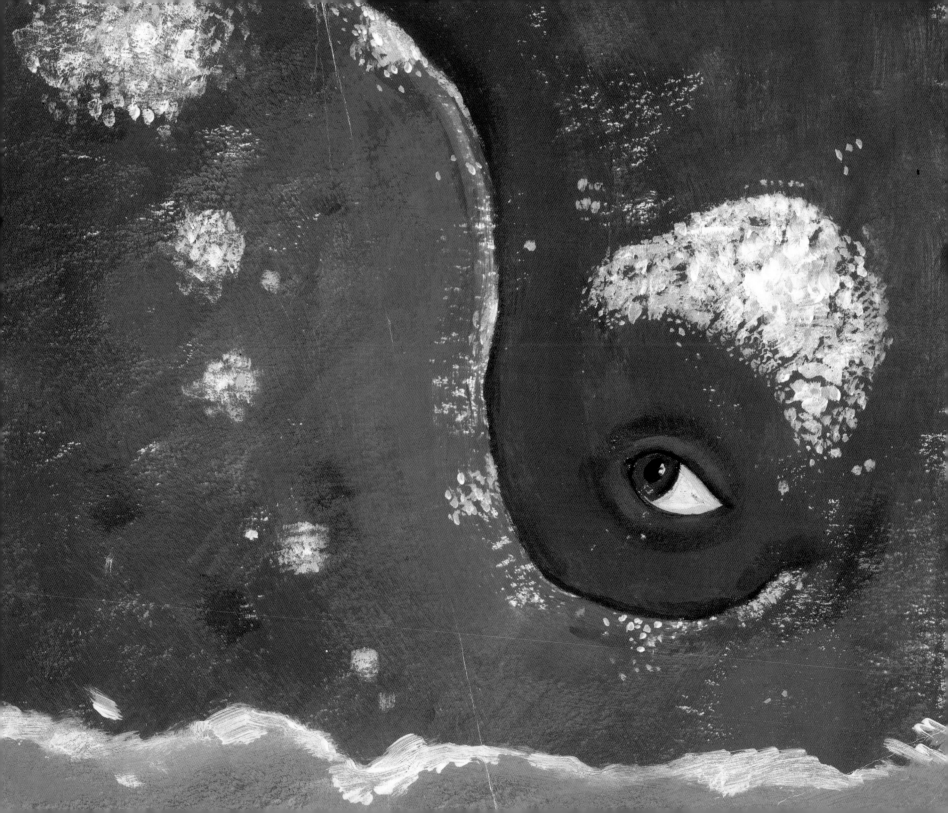

"Wow!" Dario shouts.
"Mãe, venha ver!"
Ma, come look!

SPLASH!

The whale slaps the water with his tail.
His mother hurries over.

Every day, Dario races to the beach.
Every day, the whale is there.

When Dario whistles, the whale spouts.

Dario waves, the whale breaches.

Dario watches the whale for hours.
The whale swims back and forth for hours.

"Is he your friend?"
asks the girl who made the sand castle.
Dario nods. "Yes, yes."

One day, Dario does not
go to the beach.
He has a drippy nose.
His mother puts him to bed.
"Mas!" he says. But!

The whale looks for Dario.
He waits and waits.

When Dario's nose is dry,
he rushes to the shore.
Looking. Hoping.

"They migrate," says the girl.
"They leave at the end of May."

"Não!" says Dario. No!
"He is my friend. See!"

Dario whistles.
The whale breaches.

SPLASH!

Dario runs into the water.

The whale swims close to shore. Closer than ever.

Just waves apart,
the boy and the whale stay very still,
listening and being.

"Do you have to go?" asks Dario.
The whale blinks his large dark eye.

"But you'll come back, right?"
Dario holds his breath.

He waits.
He wishes.

At last, the whale raises his great notched tail and lets it fall.

WHOOOOOOOSH!

"Okay, then," Dario says. "See you next year!"

ABOUT RIGHT WHALES

One chilly April morning, I discovered that right whale calves are just as curious as human children. While walking my dog on a Cape Cod beach, I met a baby right whale that was "skimming" only fifteen feet from the shore. When my dog barked, the whale raised its head to see who was making such a fuss. The three of us—two on the sand and one in the sea—connected, just like in the story. Afterward, the whale continued to swim along the shore, feeding, spouting, and occasionally checking on its new friends.—*CLM*

North Atlantic right whales, like Dario's whale, migrate from the coasts of Georgia and Florida to Cape Cod every spring and leave before summer. Marine biologists think that from there, they travel farther north. Whales have been spotted off the coasts of Maine and Canada in July and August. In winter, the whales migrate back to warm southern waters where pregnant females give birth to new calves. In the spring, these calves follow their mothers to Cape Cod.

North Atlantic right whale calves are a blue-gray color, and adults are black or dark gray. Whale lice, or *cyamids*, form white areas of rough skin or bumps, called *callosities*, on adults' heads and noses. These bumps form unique patterns that make individual whales easy to identify. Right whales are the only whales that have two blowholes, not one. These make a distinct *V*-shaped spray when they spout.

North Atlantic right whales are baleen whales, which means they filter plankton—microscopic animals and plants floating in the ocean—through huge baleen plates in their mouths. These plates are made of keratin, a protein found in human hair and fingernails. Although right whales occasionally scoop up food from the bottom of the ocean, they prefer to skim the sea's surface for dinner. A right whale skims by swimming with its mouth open, taking in seawater and plankton. Its baleen plates act like a strainer, trapping the food when the whale pushes the seawater back out of its mouth.

Right whales are the rarest of all whale species. Whalers in the nineteenth century used to say the whales were the "right" whales to kill because of their thick blubber, which was boiled into oil. This is where the name "right whale" comes from. So many right whales were killed that almost none were left by 1986, the year most countries agreed to stop hunting whales.

Scientists estimate that today only three to four hundred North Atlantic right whales are living in the Atlantic Ocean. Find out how you can help them and other marine animals by visiting organizations like Whale and Dolphin Conservation at www.wdcs.org.